I0456658

NEVER FORGET

A novelette by Edwina Harvey

Never Forget

NEVER FORGET

A novelette

by Edwina Harvey

 Peggy Bright Books, 2019

Never Forget

First published in Australia in 2019 by Peggy Bright Books
www.peggybrightbooks.com
Please direct all enquiries to the publisher at:
editor@peggybrightbooks.com

Other works by this author available through Peggy Bright Books:

- YA SF novel, The Whale's Tale, 2009
- SF/Urban fantasy interlinked short story collection, The Back of the Back of Beyond, 2013
- Collected writings, An Eclectic Collection of Stuff and Things, 2017

ISBN: 9780992512569

Libraries Australia ID 65054729
Science fiction, Australian.

With thanks to Ion Newcombe and Margaret Essex who helped nudge the elephant along

Cover image and internal elephant silhouette courtesy of pixabay.com

Never Forget

By Edwina Harvey

I had transcended tiredness. The long plane trip was directly followed by a long, bone-jarring ride deeper into the African wilderness in the front seat of a king cab truck that needed its suspension fixed. I was wide awake to all the new sights and sounds as I sucked gratefully at the bottled water my welcome-party had provided me with.

Michael, driving the truck, and Masego (I wanted to giggle every time I heard his name) in the back seat, were keen to show me points of interest as we journeyed further into the African bush. Flocks of birds, a few wild pigs, giraffe and zebra in the distance.

I could have – should have – arranged to spend a night resting up in Jo'burg before continuing the next leg of my pilgrimage, but I was always in a hurry, and this couldn't afford to wait.

The truck braked so unexpectedly, I almost hit the windscreen.

"Please, stay in the car. Don't look, Mma," Michael told me seriously as he signalled to Masego.

You're from Botswana, I thought absently.

I noticed they didn't lock the doors, and of course I looked – how could I not? What were they so alarmed about?

They were heading to what looked to me to be a hillock maybe four hundred metres away. I'm no good at judging distance. I noticed something moving around the mound – ears flapping, raised trunk trumpeting in defiance – a baby elephant…which meant that the mound…

Peering, I could make out four stiff legs, the fold of an ear that mimicked the continent the beast had been born on, a trunk. I could even make out the stain of black crusting blood besides the trunk where the tusk had been hacked out of its head. No doubt there was a similar wound on the other side of its face.

I looked away, best to concentrate on what Michael and Masego were doing.

I smiled; they seemed to be playing 'tag' with the baby elephant. It would alternately charge at them, then retreat behind the mass of its dead mother, touching her with its trunk as if imploring her to get up so they could run to safety together.

Tears sprang in my sleep-deprived eyes and I pushed open the car door, walked towards the carnage.

Michael noticed me and called, "Go back to the truck, please. You are not safe."

"What are you trying to do?"

"If we can capture the baby elephant, we can take him with us."

Oh sure. Of course. Easy. Not.

Masego and Michael tried to get closer, and there was another mock charge from the baby pachyderm. We could be doing this all day!

"Why don't we all stand still?" I suggested. "Let's see what happens." I didn't know much about elephant psychology, but it could work sometimes with cats and horses, and surely a baby elephant could be no more fickle than a cat?

So we three played at being statues.

The elephant calf hid behind his mother's corpse, laid his trunk across her stiff body and made sad, imploring noises that broke my heart.

"She's not coming back, little one. Your Mamma's gone. And to you, we look like the things that killed her, don't we?"

I hadn't realised I'd spoken out loud until Michael and Masego both glanced at me, worried. Damn the fogginess of sleep deprivation. I hadn't even realised I'd brought my bottle of water with me when I'd got out of the truck, but now I noticed it I took a swig; the sun was hot and I was dehydrated.

The grieving baby elephant got the scent of the water. His trunk raised up like a submarine's periscope and he sniffed the air. He was thirsty. How long had he stood, keeping watch over his mother's body? Had he tried to suckle from her? Death's not an easy concept to come to grips with when you're still getting used to being alive.

I stretched out my arm and shook the water bottle enticingly, but my feet didn't move at all. I wasn't going to chase him, I wasn't going to advance then retreat the way the men had done. If I was still, he might get curious and come right up to me. That's the way it sometimes works with cats and horses.

But he was neither of those. Cautiously, he emerged from his dead mother's shadow, then charged full-tilt towards me. I squealed and bolted for the safety of the truck cabin, glancing back when I was safely within to notice Masego and Michael had followed him.

"That was good, Mma. We've got him where we want him now."

The little pachyderm had skidded to a stop four metres from the truck. He made a frustrated noise in my direction. He still wanted the water.

"What do we do now?" I called to my guides, but Masego was already dragging two very solid-looking planks of wood from the tray at the back of the truck.

"We use the water to entice him up the ramp and into the truck," he told me.

Of course we do. What could be simpler? I got out of the truck, shook my water bottle again and instantly had the baby elephant's interest.

"Let me help you up into the tray, Mma." Masego gallantly took my hand as I walked up the impromptu ramp he'd constructed, but if any of us was expecting the baby to just walk right up we were all sadly mistaken.

Leaning back against the cab, I offered the water bottle again. The baby wanted the water, but had already learned humans weren't to be trusted. Michael and Masego formed a "V" a safe distance behind him. The trick was to make it his idea to scramble up the ramp, but it was going to be a battle of wills and patience.

It was a stand-off. The elephant calf would put a foot on the ramp to get to the water, then reconsider and shuffle back a few steps. Time ticked away and we were all hot and exasperated. The baby flapped his ears to cool himself down, but he was beginning to fade – looking tired and sad.

I could sympathise. What I wouldn't give for a shower and a nearby bed to fall into right now. I took a swig from the water bottle and the baby elephant exploded into action, bellowing and coming at me full tilt up the ramp. Masego and Michael were yelling at me and each other, but I had my own problems, suddenly up close and personal with the baby who didn't seem so small when he was this close. I could have scrambled over the roof of the cab, but that seemed like a cop-out as I'd been the one who'd been teasing him up here all along.

His trunk was raised back onto his forehead like a question mark, his mouth was open, and the noises he made were ones of wanting. I poured some water into his mouth, most of it fell out the sides, but he shut his mouth, capturing the remains as Masego climbed over the back of the tray, a coil of rope slung over his shoulder. The calf barely noticed, he was fixated on the water, his mouth open again, wanting more. This time I got the bottle closer and he clamped onto it while his trunk wrapped around my arm and he sucked so hard that I felt the tug all the way back to my shoulder.

The plastic bottle crumpled, empty and dry, and the elephant let it and my hand go, but the sensitive tip of his trunk explored my arm, wanting more.

Michael appeared at the side of the truck, another nearly full water bottle in his hand. The calf sucked greedily at that too, but I doubted we'd have enough water to sate him.

Masego was using his rope to weave a light harness around the baby elephant – a loop around his waist, behind his back legs and around his neck to encourage him to stay in the truck, tying the rope to D rings on the chassis. He and Michael worked in unison as if this sort of thing happened every day for them.

"What now?" I wondered out loud.

"Now we all go home." Michael's smile was as bright and wide as the sun as he climbed back into the truck cab.

"We're not getting back in?" I asked Masego, slightly alarmed.

"You can if you want, Mma, but I will stay with the baby elephant."

"Then I will too," I decided, hoping I didn't end up being thrown out of the truck if it went over a bump.

The truck moved off slowly and carefully. Whether that was because of the extra ballast it was carrying, I couldn't be sure.

After an alarmed toot as the truck lurched forward, the baby elephant seemed to accept the idea of moving without having to do the hard work himself, just as he didn't seem to mind a loose rope harness holding him in place.

Maybe the swaying and bouncing of the truck even lulled him into restfulness. He seemed to take it all calmly, and after a while he sat down in the tray, making a low noise. Like a blind man groping, his trunk sought my arm and wrapped around my wrist like he might grab at his mother's trunk, or tail, to stay in contact with her. He seemed to relax, his eyes even half-closed, though the low rumbling continued. Masego smiled at me. "I think he's snoring."

It was late afternoon when we reached our destination. The Scientist I'd come all this way to see was standing on the wide veranda, hands locked solid on the handrails, eyes set in our direction. He was as I'd imagined him: unassuming, decked out in beiges and greens to blend with the landscape. His face was protected by a wide-brimmed hat, even though the veranda offered shade.

"I was getting worried that something had happened," he called out as we got close, then he caught sight of the calf in the back of the truck. "I wasn't expecting you to bring your work with you!" He seemed amused, maybe a little puzzled.

As we pulled up in front of the house, Masego jumped over the side of the flatbed saying, "I will go and get some milk for the baby."

The Scientist strode down the stairs to meet us as Michael got out of the truck's cabin. "We found him on the way, Rra. About twenty kilometres from here. His mother had been slaughtered."

With all this activity, the baby elephant stirred, got to his feet, realised he was restrained and seemed to be about to throw an almighty tantrum, but Masego reappeared with two large plastic bottles with long rubber teats attached. The elephant fixated on the bottles.

"How do we get him out of the truck, Masego?"

"The same way we got him in, Mma." He passed me a bottle that was almost knocked out of my hand by the baby pachyderm in his eagerness to drink. Meanwhile, Masego lowered the tail gate of the truck and dragged out those two sturdy planks to create a ramp. I hadn't noticed him put them back in the truck once we'd got the elephant in.

The calf sucked greedily at the milk as Masego loosened the rope harness around him.

"No problem getting him to drink then," the Scientist noted dryly, looking the calf over. "Looks like he's a keeper."

When the first bottle of formula was drained, Masego used the second one to tempt the elephant out of the truck. The calf was able to turn around on the flat bed and he made it down the ramp in a hurry, outstretched trunk reaching for the full milk bottle as he trumpeted.

I staggered out of the truck, the world moving beneath me, and introduced myself to the Scientist.

"Yes, I know who you are, I've been expecting you," he reminded me kindly. "You must have had a long trip, you're looking very tired. Would you care to see your room? You probably want to freshen up."

He took my bag out of the back of the king cab.

So he doubled as a porter? Neat.

I followed him towards the house. When I looked back over my shoulder to see how 'my' baby elephant was doing, I caught the Scientist doing the same, concern in his pale blue eyes. He had a heart then. It mattered to me that he had a heart.

My room was cool, dark and inviting. A cream lace bedspread and matching curtains. The knotted mosquito net above the bed was a necessity rather than romantic whimsy here.

"Your bathroom's just there," the Scientist indicated another doorway. I nodded, thanked him, out of adrenalin, empty and tired.

"I'll leave you to rest, then. See you at dinner, perhaps?"

I didn't even hear him depart. I don't even remember unknotting the mosquito net or getting into bed.

I resurfaced five hours later, having missed dinner, but food had been kept for me and the Scientist was waiting.

"How's the elephant calf?" was the first thing I wanted to know.

"He's asleep in one of the stables. Or he was when I checked on him about an hour ago. Masego's spending the night with him."

"They hacked the tusks out of his mother's head, but I couldn't see that they'd taken any of the meat. Not that I'd condone the hunting if they had, but I know the country's in drought."

The Scientist nodded. "And a resource is a resource. I doubt the mother was killed by a local, or even a poacher. We have a new problem in Africa. The Chinese throw their money at us; come in and build the infrastructure that we so desperately need. They're building a multi-lane freeway not thirty kilometres from here. The engineers, project managers, construction supervisors and the likes all come out from China. They see the ivory on the hoof, and it's too much temptation for some of them. They go elephant hunting."

"And they're allowed?" I said, askance.

He considered his answer, "They're not actively pursued. They're worth too much to the country."

"And so are elephants! How many millions of dollars and employment opportunities are generated by tourists coming to see the Big 5 each year?"

He nodded wisely, his voice calm and quiet in contrast to my explosion. "I know. We're on the same side, remember?"

Of course. That's why I'd come all this way to meet him. We'd spoken on the phone and on Skype, sent emails to and fro discussing his work. He needed funding to continue his research, but I wanted to meet him face to face before I committed.

"So tell me about your research," I suggested.

"What, now? You don't want to wait until morning?"

But I was alert now, the jetlag momentarily thrown aside. "Now is good." Before the next wave of weariness swallowed me.

He took me at my word, took me to his office, proceeded to lecture me on genetics and gene splicing, how it had worked with simpler species, even domestic animals, so why not this? He showed me graphs and presentations off the internet on his laptop and all that registered with me was that they had wi-fi out here.

Finally he stopped, regarded me kindly and said, "You're looking glassy-eyed. Is any of this going in?"

"Not a lot," I admitted.

"Okay. Do you want the short version again?" he offered.

I already knew the short version. That's why I'd come here. All this way...they had wi-fi here? I really needed more sleep. "Tell me the short version again."

"Elephants are hunted for their ivory tusks. Elephants are at risk of extinction because they've been hunted almost to the point where they can't sustain or regenerate their populations."

I nodded. This was familiar territory.

"Elephants also differ from many other mammals in that they replace their chewing teeth six times during their lives, the new teeth grow in at the back of the mouth and move forward, pushing the old ones out."

"Sharks teeth do that," I commented. I think I just wanted to prove I was paying attention.

He nodded, then pointed his index finger skyward. "*But,* their tusks are just modified incisors. If I can tweak their genes into recognising that their tusks are also teeth, they should – at least in theory – start shedding their tusks every eight to ten years. The new tusks, emerging from the hollow part of the tusk embedded in the elephant's head, will push out the older tusks."

"Don't they add more layers of ivory to the inside of the tusk every year?"

He seemed impressed by my knowledge. "That's right. And the weight of the solid part of the tusk should help it to break away as it's pushed out by the new tusk."

"But what happens to the nerve that runs down the tusk?"

There was a slight uplift to the corners of his mouth. I think he was surprised that I knew this stuff. Heck, *I* was surprised that I knew this stuff! I must have read it somewhere, but I couldn't remember where.

"With a bit of tweaking, it can be encouraged to disintegrate as the new tusk pushes through. And that will also help the old tusk drop off."

"Hmmm. But elephants use their tusks as tools – for digging for salt or water, for stripping bark off trees; even to defend themselves."

It was like he'd been waiting for me to say this and I'd just proved myself a clever pupil.

"Well, the new tusks will already be growing out, so they won't be totally tusk-less, but if we can perfect the regrowth of the tusks aspect, possibly we can tweak things further so the tusk on one side of the head falls off in one cycle, and the tusk on the opposite side of the head falls off the next. But that's a long way off."

"It'd mean a lot of asymmetrical elephants running around the place," I commented, picturing lopsided pachyderms in my mind.

"Better than no elephants at all," he reminded me.

I had to agree with that.

"If we can make ivory a renewable resource then elephants are more valuable alive than dead. Ivory becomes a harvestable commodity. Keep the elephants alive there's the opportunity to collect more ivory from them - and collect it more safely than killing an elephant to take its ivory once. QED fewer elephants will be shot."

"At least in theory," I reminded him. There'd still be confrontations with farmers as herds raided or trampled crops, and those who weren't prepared to wait for the elephant to shed its tusk, or who wanted a hunting trophy.

"At least in theory," he concurred.

It sounded so easy to do, just jigger the genetics; but I knew he'd already been researching this on and off for more than a decade and he hadn't got all the ducks to line up in a row yet.

He might have been under-funded, but I had deep pockets and a love of animals. Besides, I thought he was kinda cute.

He couldn't supress a yawn, and my next wave of tiredness began to hit. It was 3am, time to go back to bed.

At least I was able to crawl out of bed in time for breakfast later that morning.

Over cups of tea the Scientist admitted he was surprised I travelled alone. He'd expected an entourage.

"It's easier on my own. Besides, I brought you an elephant, didn't I?"

He smiled at that. "Masego tells me the calf slept most of the night and seems to be settling in nicely. He's volunteered for nanny-duty. He'll stay close to the calf, be a familiar face for it in a strange world"

"When can I see my elephant?"

Yes, I knew he wasn't strictly mine, but you don't spend time getting bumped and rocked around in the back of a truck with a small pachyderm holding your hand without feeling some bond.

"I was planning on giving you a tour of the complex after breakfast if you'd like? You can see him after that?"

"Good, let's go." Always in a hurry, that's me.

We got into a jeep and drove into the African wilderness.

He found his big old bull called "George" and explained because George was mostly wild and dangerous, we'd view his small herd from a safe distance. George had a pair of the longest curved tusks I'd seen on an elephant. And then I'd only seen them in photos of hunting parties with their trophies, taken in the early part of the last century. He'd be worth a poacher's fortune if they ever found him. His two concubines – Maisy and Daphne - were similarly well endowed in the ivory department.

All three carried scars from previous encounters with poachers and were lucky to be alive. Here they were mostly left alone to roam the double-fenced bushland of the property.

Maisy was the matriarch of the tiny herd that consisted of her, Daphne and an adolescent called Arabella, another foundling, probably about 5 years old. As we headed back to the homestead, the Scientist let slip that he thought Daphne was pregnant to George, and he was keen to see what the next generation of his project would yield.

The tour continued when we got back to the homestead. The stables the Scientist had spoken of were built to elephant proportions, making for a very tall, very wide stable block with very roomy compartments. The corral in the compound was fenced with large vertical logs, with gaps between them wide enough so we could see through, but the animals couldn't get out. It held two more elephant calves and…

"Are they antelope?" I asked.

"Fallow deer."

"They keep the elephants company?" I guessed.

"They also shed their horns annually – well, at least the males do. They were part of my early research, but it never went anywhere."

"So why isn't my little fellow in there with those calves?" I asked, knowing elephants were herd animals.

"He will be soon enough. Two weeks quarantine first. It will give him a chance to settle in, gain a little confidence, grow a little more. He's a lot younger than those two, and they might play rough. Let's go see how he's doing."

Masego had my calf in a garden area not far from the corral so he could hear and smell the other calves. When he heard us approaching, the calf swung around to face us, then charged towards me. The Scientist tried to pull me to safety, but I didn't feel in danger.

The calf made a joyful toot, stopped a metre from me and reached for me with his little trunk. I stretched my arm out to meet him and he blew gently into the palm of my hand before wrapping his trunk around my wrist. I looked into his eyes and saw recognition there. I was part of his new family.

"Hello, my little man. Are you okay? Did Masego look after you last night?"

"He slept well, Mma. Yesterday was a big day for him."

"Yes it was, wasn't it? A very sad day for my poor Sweet William," I said as I stroked his bristly head.

I heard the Scientist choke behind me, then mutter, "You can't call him that. That's *my* name."

I did a double take. "I wondered why it sounded familiar. But everyone calls you Bill."

"Yes, but still…" he blustered.

"They'll know it's not you. You two don't look a thing alike." I grinned, but he had no comeback. I'd won.

Sweet William and I went on to indulge in a mud-bath, with Masego and the Scientist trying but failing to stay mud-free. I had to shower and change, the maid tut-tutting as she took my mud-caked outfit away to try to wash clean.

Sweet William had followed Masego back to his stable to have lunch then doze away the heat of the afternoon sun. I wished I could do the same, but the Scientist, bless him, was dedicated to impressing me with more of his research, naively presuming I hadn't researched him before I'd first made contact with him. I knew he'd written his post-doc on elephants shedding their tusks, but his published papers were all on more mundane subjects. He was a quiet crusader; very little of his research into elephants was in the public domain.

As the afternoon wore on, during a break in his well-rehearsed presentation I asked: "Can we go look for cheetahs now?" I must have sounded like a bored tourist, only here to see the sights and play with the orphaned elephants. Well, I guess in a way I was that.

He looked at me, nonplussed. "But I haven't finished my presentation yet."

"I know. But you've got your funding. I was 90% sure I was going to fund your research before I got on the plane. I just wanted to see the work you are doing for myself to be 100% certain. Despite what you might think, I do work hard for my money, you know. And I just don't throw it away on anything."

He was flustered now. "I assure you that – "

But I waved him into silence, let the fifth ace fall from my sleeve. "By the way, when were you planning on telling me about adding the mammoth genes to the mix? Those three mature elephants we saw today seem to be a success story."

My stare was fixed like a cobra on its prey, and he was so stunned he actually fell into the nearest chair. He hadn't published that part of his research; probably didn't even talk about it to his colleagues because it was private.

I had him. He was really disconcerted now. "Who? How did you - ?"

I raised an eyebrow at him. At least he didn't try to deny it. Honesty was important to me. "No one told me. I made a calculated guess. No one's recorded an African elephant with tusks that long in more than eighty years."

"You're very astute."

"And very rich. And I want to support you. What will one million a year get me?"

"My eternal gratitude and I'll name my first born after you?"

I caught the glint of humour in his eyes. We'd reached a new milestone in our relationship. The feeling of *You're alright* was mutual.

"Well, I've already named my baby elephant after you," I conceded. "Shall we?" I whipped out my smart phone to make the transaction, glad they had wi-fi here.

He checked his bank balance on his laptop soon after, trying hard to supress his surprised delight.

"Now can we go play tourist? I've come a long way."

The worst of the midday heat was over. The sun was on its downward march as he took me on a safari of the wider area including the river, where he pointed out a cheetah to me. It was so well camouflaged I never would have seen it on my own. The hippos bathing in the river were easier to spot. We got lucky and saw some more giraffe and zebra. I took lots of photos and began to unwind into holiday mode. And why not? My work here was done. I'd made my mind up about the Scientist and sponsored his research for a year. I could have rebooked my flight, headed back to the rat race right away, but I was feeling good about myself and figured I deserved a bit of time off. Besides, I wanted to hang around for a bit to see how my Sweet William was settling in. Alright then, I wanted to stay and play.

I always knew when Sweet William was hungry – he'd try to grab my breast with his trunk instead of reaching for my hand, and Masego – his usual companion - would turn away, embarrassed.

Not surprisingly, the Scientist and I talked more about elephants. The truth was despite their status with tourists, elephants were considered a hindrance by a lot of Africans, raiding farmlands and destroying villages, especially in times of drought when two legged and four all went hungry. The number of wild elephants was declining so fast, the Scientist wasn't even sure if they'd go extinct before he knew if his gene manipulation worked. It was a race against time. And ivory hunters.

It hurt me to leave. I wanted to stay in this little oasis in Africa, conveniently connected to the rest of the world by wi-fi, yet away from it all, but my Real Life was calling me back to 'civilization'.

"Can I come visit you next year?" I asked the Scientist. "Check for myself how you're progressing?"

"Of course you can! You have an open invitation whenever you want. And I promise I'll keep you updated so you know how your money's being spent."

"I'll hold you to that."

Masego had brought Sweet William to say good-bye, and that was the hardest rift of all because I felt most connected to the little elephant. Wished I could take him with me in fact; but in the space of a couple of weeks I'd seen him transform from scared, starving orphaned calf to well-fed, cheeky and playful. He'd grown so much in that short space of time. I knew he was safe here. In a few days he'd be allowed to meet with the other calves through the safety of the fence, touch another elephant for the first time in weeks, form new friendships. I'd miss that milestone and many others I wanted so much to see, so why was I going?

But Michael was waiting to drive me back to the airport in the same truck that brought me and Sweet William here. So I went.

At the airport as Michael handed me my bag he pressed something else into my hand, smiling. "A present, Mma, from Sweet William to you."

I looked at the elephant charm strung with some beads on a simple cord bracelet and the walls I'd been keeping so carefully in place while I'd said my farewells at the compound and during the long drive to the airport came tumbling down. I hugged Michael to me with a strength I didn't know I had, with absolutely no regard for protocol. Emotion cracked my voice as I told him, "Thank you. And thank Masego, and the Scientist and Sweet William for me. I'll miss you all so very, very much."

He patted my back, and as I leaned away from him I saw his tear-welled eyes. I was as wanted among them as my baby elephant.

When he spoke his voice was as emotion-cracked as mine. "Come back to us, Mma, whenever you can. You have family here."

We turned from each other to depart, but as we did our curved fingertips interlocked briefly – like two trunks curved around each other.

First class wasn't overly crowded, but the flight was spoiled by the trophy hunter loudly bragging how he'd spent a fortune to shoot a lion in a game park reserved for 'sport', and how he was worried now that he wouldn't get its mounted head past customs. Such were the worries of the uber-rich!

The Scientist was true to his word, sending me regular updates on his research, and images of Sweet William's progress. He'd integrated well with the other calves and spent his days with them in the big corral. My little elephant was growing at a cracking pace.

I couldn't fully keep my end of the bargain though. Sending money to fund the research was never going to be a problem, but as much as the Scientist reminded me that I had an open invitation there, I could never seem to find the time in my busy schedule to get back to Africa, as much as I wanted to. An elephant charm always worn on my right wrist was the closest I got to a real elephant for more than two years.

Eventually it was Sweet William who had me charging back to Africa in dramatic circumstances.

The Scientist phoned me and after a quick salutation, he dived straight into the problem, as was his style.

"Has it made your news yet?" he asked me.

"Has what? Have you finally had a breakthrough?" I was suddenly excited.

"Nothing that good, I'm afraid. Look, there's been an incident with your elephant." Calling him 'Sweet William' on our skype calls always made him cringe, so it was usually 'my elephant'.

I heard the seriousness in his voice as a litany of perils ran through my head: anthrax, tetanus, poachers, lions…

"What's happened?"

"We had poachers cut both the fences and break in –"

And Sweet William and the other youngsters had joined George's herd 8 months ago

"A few elephants got out, including Sweet William."

"Oh God!"

"He hasn't come to any harm yet," the Scientist hastened to add, but I noted the pause before he said "yet".

"Bill, what's happened?" I didn't often call him by name, but I needed his attention now. I needed to know.

"He charged one of those open-air tourist vans, you know the ones?"

Did it bloody matter if I knew or not? He was stalling for time, trying to prepare me for the worst.

"He trampled a Korean tourist – pulled him right out of the truck and –"

He wouldn't have said 'Korean' if it hadn't been important, but my mind was trying to deal with too many things to process it. "Don't they carry guns on those trucks? To protect the tourists in case anything like this happens. Is that what you're trying to tell me, Bill? They shot Sweet William?"

"They fired their guns, yes, and that scared him off; at least far enough that they could get the poor guy back to safety. He's suffered broken ribs and concussion. Frankly he's very lucky to be alive. But the media are all over this. If you haven't heard it yet, you will soon. I thought I'd better tell you first. They're calling him a rogue elephant and demanding he be killed."

"Have you told them he's a vital part of your experiment?" I asked.

"They haven't worked that piece of the puzzle out yet, no, and I'm loath to tell them, because that really would be setting the cat amongst the pigeons: 'Experiment goes horribly wrong', 'Mad Scientist Engineers Rampaging Elephant'. I have no idea how to keep a lid on this."

"Where is he now?" I asked.

"Back safe in the compound with Coco and Akuchi. But I really need your help on this one, PR is not my thing at all."

"I'll be there as soon as I can." And this time I meant it.

I was on the first plane to Africa, dragging a PA, a couple of consultants and a lawyer with me.

The news of the tourist being trampled by an elephant was a grab on the inflight news. I instantly recognised Sweet William on the screen as I distractedly toyed with my elephant charm bracelet.

I put through calls to various animal welfare agencies and African politicians to brief them of the potential problem. Despite anticipated public backlash, that elephant had to live at all costs. He was a vital part of a ground-breaking experiment that was nearing completion. Alright, so I bent those facts quite a bit. I'd straighten them out later.

By the time the plane touched down we'd worked out our best line of defence and various contingency plans. The Scientist wouldn't like being forced to disclose his studies now before he had any proof to show the media. They'd call him a crackpot, his reputation would be ruined. We'd only use his work as a defence if we really had to, but judging from the media coverage I was seeing, we'd really have to.

Michael and Masego were my welcome party at the airport, but they'd been expecting a party of one, like last time, and were quite taken aback by the entourage I brought with me this time.

"How is he?" I asked my guides, and they didn't have to ask which one I was enquiring about.

Michael answered, "He is fine, Mma. He does not know he has done anything wrong."

"The Scientist is also well," Masego chimed in, smiling brightly.

They were both pleased to see me, but I think we all wished it was a happier home-coming.

There wasn't enough seating in the cab of the truck for all of us, so my intrepid PA and Masego rode in the tray with the luggage. They'd all brought too much luggage, unsure of where they were going or for how long.

I still couldn't see the importance of it being a Korean national Sweet William had attacked until we were driving on the smooth multi-lane highway that had been built by the Chinese.

I kept my voice low as I asked, "Michael, do you think Sweet William remembered what the person who killed his mother looked like?"

"Who can say, Mma? But it would seem..." He gave me a side-long glance, as if the others in the cab would scoff at him if he said it, but I would know the truth.

When we finally reached the compound (the trip there seemed to take forever, and this time we didn't have the distraction of finding an orphaned elephant calf to contend with), my introductions were brusque to the point of being rude, but the Scientist seemed to forgive me as his people ushered my people and their luggage into the homestead.

I only had to glance at him for Bill to read my mind. "He's this way." He gestured towards the corral, and I hurried ahead of him. His hand was forceful on mine as I went to open the gate. "No. We must presume he's dangerous. You can't go in with him."

But at least I could look at him through the wide gaps between the vertical logs of the corral fencing.

The three young elephants had been standing in the shade to avoid the midday sun, large ears flapping to cool their blood.

"They're all so grown up," I commented.

Recognising my voice, Sweet William turned around, gave a short trumpet and took hurried steps towards me. He pressed his head against the corral posts and put his trunk through the gap.

"You remember me?" I was surprised, despite all I'd heard. It had only been for two weeks two years ago.

"They never forget," the Scientist said. "But be careful."

But what was there to be careful of? This was the same Sweet William I'd fed and played with, only much bigger, more mature. I'd known him the instant I'd seen him on the media reports, and he knew me. His trunk waved to me through the posts and I held out my hand. He explored it gently, blowing softly into my palm. Then his trunk wrapped around my wrist and the elephant charm bracelet there as we two long-lost friends reconnected.

I hadn't expected to cry as I told my elephant, "I didn't mean to be away so long. Really I didn't. But I'm here now…I'm here now." I stroked his upper trunk with my free hand and he made little happy toots and rumbles.

"He's happy to see you too," the Scientist told me, his hand on my shoulder.

"His tusks are growing out," I noticed. They were maybe already nine inches long.

"All three of the calves have the mammoth tusk splice in their DNA as well as the code-tinkering for their tusks to fall out at a given trigger point, but it's yet to happen with old George, and he's been my first guinea pig for all the trials. I don't know what I'm doing wrong, I thought I'd have solved the problem by now."

I caught the self-recriminatory look on his face, as if African elephants would become extinct because of his failings.

"Come on," I told him. "Let's get back to the house and plot our defence. The press will be at your doorstep before you know it."

The dining room was awash with sound bites.

"If I was any good at public speaking, I'd have been a lecturer." That was from the Scientist when my PA and PR people had suggested what he might say.

"We play down the mammoth genes angle, otherwise they'll be accusing you of being Frankenstein."

"Thank God that elephant didn't kill the Korean tourist."

"We've already compensated and repatriated him."

"But the fact that he thought the tourist was the same nationality as the people who shot his mother makes this a real human-interest story. I'm sure it will work in our favour."

"I've got all major animal welfare groups on our side. If they suggest we have to euthanize the animal, there'll be a public outcry."

In many countries of the world, maybe. But in Africa humans were regularly having clashes with elephants. Usually it didn't end well for the elephants.

"I've drafted a statement to be read out to the press."

Then Abebe, the maid, entered the dining room looking flustered. She addressed the Scientist: "Rra, there are four land rovers coming down the road. You must come quickly."

We all hustled out on to the veranda to meet them.

As I was expecting, the journalists were leading the way, not the authorities to demand justice.

The Scientist looked like he was going to be sick. "I am so not ready for this," he moaned.

"Give it your best shot. And I'll be there to back you up any way I can." I squeezed his arm.

The questions flew thick and fast, but we got in quick with the human-interest story of how Sweet William had been found as an orphaned calf next to the corpse of his dead mother, slaughtered for her ivory. We tried to steer away from the ethnic background of her killers, but that was the lead one of the journalists was determined to take. There'd been Chinese in the area building the new freeway when this elephant had been found as a calf, hadn't there? Was it possible that the elephant saw a racial similarity in the Korean tourist he'd pulled out of the truck? (*Where the heck had she dug that up from?*)

Oh, we had to dance around that one lightly! How do you know what goes on in the mind of a young orphaned elephant? We could only speculate, we said hesitantly. There'd be diplomatic outrage if this angle got published, that's for sure.

We tried to stick to the story we wanted to tell. The tourist had been repatriated and compensated, the Scientist told the press. He was very sorry for the unfortunate incident, but the elephants wouldn't have escaped if the property's double fencing hadn't been cut by poachers.

Bill was getting flustered by all their questions, so I stepped up and tried to steer the journalists towards the good-news story we were trying to sell: how the Scientist was trying to perfect a way for ivory to be regenerated. But then they started asking if Sweet William was a crazed experiment gone wrong. Wouldn't it be best if this rogue elephant was shot? Bill looked as uncomfortable as I felt. The story was heading in exactly the direction we didn't want it to take. This was all going to hell in a handbasket!

Then I looked up and saw two young men lumbering across the plain towards us, smiling broadly, carrying something large, curved, heavy and white between them. As they got closer they began calling to the Scientist.

"Mr William! Mr William!"

This confused the journalists. Wasn't that the elephant's name? "Told you you should have called your elephant something else," the Scientist told me out of the corner of his mouth.

"Old George has dropped his tusk!" announced one of the panting runners.

The Scientist whooped, picked me up and whirled me around, smiling from ear to ear. Stunned by his exuberance, it took me a moment to understand what this meant, then I realised we'd won the lottery. It worked! We had the proof we needed. And it couldn't have come at a better time!

The young lads cut a swathe through the cluster of journalists and presented the tusk like a trophy to the Scientist. On end, the tusk was taller than the Scientist was.

The journalists had all fallen silent, and now the Scientist addressed them confidently, "Ladies and gentlemen, this is what I've been working towards since I wrote my post-doc: a way to genetically modify elephants so they lose their tusks on an average of once every eight years or so only to have new tusks grow again. This is proof that we've turned ivory into a renewable commodity. Ivory can now be collected without risking human or elephant lives. You'll all be familiar with how elephants grow and replace their chewing teeth six times during their lives?"

By the looks on their faces it was obvious they weren't, but he pressed on regardless. "Tusks are the elephant's incisor teeth grown large. I've simply switched on the gene that will make them fall out as if they were chewing teeth. The old tusk will be pushed out by another new tusk growing underneath it."

He'd failed to tell them that "simply switched on the gene" had taken decades of research to perfect, but that didn't matter.

The reporters silently digested what he'd told them for a moment, then we were barraged with different questions.

Renewable ivory? Maybe six sets of tusks during the life of each elephant? Just follow the elephants and collect the tusks as they shed?

"This young elephant, and others like him, was orphaned when his mother was killed for her ivory," the Scientist reminded them. "He and his herd-mates are the second generation of the experiment, yes. They've had their genes manipulated since they were all young calves. When they're old enough to breed, it is hoped the tusk-shedding genes will be passed on naturally to their progeny. As you know, the demand for ivory has only risen over the years, with many now advocating to sell it openly to quash the black-market trade. I hope I've perfected a sustainable way to meet that demand, and to save the African elephant from extinction."

Elephants confronting humans was nothing new. An elephant attacking a tourist was more unusual, and that was the story they'd all come here to get. But a scientist perfecting renewable ivory - well, that was a BIG NEWS story; a story you didn't read about every day, a story that would be heard and read all around the world. And they all wanted a piece of it.

The Scientists hadn't seen it yet, but I could see how their minds had shifted. Already there was shuffling in the pack of journalists, requests for photos of him and interviews. Whereas they'd all been wanting photos of Sweet William before, the Scientist and renewable ivory were their centre of attention now. So far the Scientist was coping, comfortable talking about his research and what it might mean. This exposure would bring him more funding, other scientists wanting to join his research. As long as he didn't stumble, as long as the journalists didn't try to bring him down.

To save my elephant, I'd thrown the Scientist to the lions, but he was doing fine.

And I was sure Sweet William would gladly relinquish the spotlight.

About the author:

Edwina Harvey is a writer, editor, silk painter and ceramic artist.

Her short stories and articles have appeared in a variety of publications including *Aurealis, Antipodean SF, Grass Roots, Harbinger, Magpies, Strange Pleasures #3* and *Worlds Next Door*

Edwina's previous books, *The Whale's Tale, The Back of the Back of Beyond,* and *An Eclectic Collection of Stuff and Things* were published through Peggy Bright Books. (www.peggybrightbooks.com)

She was a founding member of *Andromeda Spaceways Inflight Magazine,* which rekindled her love of editing. Edwina received her editing qualifications in 2012 and now works as a freelance editor, specialising in editing speculative fiction.

Never Forget is a prequel to her short story, *When Whales Cry (first published in Potato Monkey, 2003, reprinted in The Whale's Tale e-book and Eclectic Collection of Stuff and Things.)*

She shares a love for animals with the protagonist, but alas, doesn't have her deep pockets.

Peggy Bright Books. Proudly celebrating 10 years of publishing square pegs for round hole, 2019.

www.ingramcontent.com/pod-product-compliance
Lightning Source LLC
Chambersburg PA
CBHW020144150626

46552CB00021B/1649